The Emperor's New Clones

JONATHAN
EM̶̶̶̶̶̶̶̶̶̶̶̶

MARTIN
C̶H̶A̶T̶T̶E̶RTON

For Otter Class
of Round Hill Primary School,
for being such excellent illustrators
J.E.

To Grandad Edwin Marshall, from Nat
(via Martin)
M.C.

EGMONT
We bring stories to life

Book Band: Lime

First published in Great Britain 2015
by Egmont UK Ltd
The Yellow Building, 1 Nicholas Road, London W11 4AN
Text copyright © Jonathan Emmett
Illustrations copyright © Martin Chatterton
The author and illustrator have asserted their moral rights.
ISBN 9781405275408
A CIP catalogue record for this title is available from the British Library
58740/1

Contents

Red Bananas

Through to the Final!

There was just one minute left until the end of the Junior League semi-final match, and the score was nine all.

'Pass it to Robbie!' shouted Barney, the Comets' team captain.

Alicia flew over the other players and fired the blasterball between the two Dog-Star defenders. Both defenders lunged for the ball, but before they could reach it, Robbie Remus zoomed towards them.

He caught the blasterball in his glove and fired it back out again. The ball hurtled through the air, just clear of the hole-keeper's outstretched glove.

Then it vanished into the Dog-Stars' black hole.

The whistle went for the end of the match.

Alicia flew up and high-fived Robbie so hard that it sent him spinning head over heels into the curved wall of the court.

'Nice shot, Robbie!' she said.

Robbie hit the 'off' button on his anti-gravity harness and dropped down to join the rest of his team.

'That was close,' said Barney, shaking his head, but he was grinning as much as the others.

'What are you complaining about?' said Robbie. 'We're through to the final!'

It had been the Comets' best season ever.

The whole team was thrilled that they had made it all the way to the Junior League Final next month. But no one was happier than Robbie. He was the Comets' youngest player but their top scorer.

When Robbie wasn't playing blasterball, he was thinking about it. He had his whole life planned out. He was going to become a professional player for one of the big teams and go all the way to the Galactic Cup Final.

But for now he just wanted to help the Comets win the Junior League.

The Luck of the Draw

The next day, Robbie was watching the news with his mum and dad.

'Her Majesty the Empress of the Galaxy, ruler of the United Planets, passed away peacefully in her sleep last night,' announced the newsreader with a tear in her eye.

The Empress had been very old, so the news was sad, but not surprising.

'Any moment now, we will have the results of the draw for the new Empress or Emperor,' the newsreader went on.

'What does she mean by "draw"?' asked Robbie.

'Whenever an Empress or Emperor dies, a new one is chosen in a draw,' explained Dad. 'It could be anybody in the whole Empire!'

'It might be someone from Alpha Regulon!' said Mum, excitedly.

'It won't be,' said Robbie. 'Nobody from our planet ever gets picked for anything.'

'Citizens of the Empire,' said the newsreader, 'your new Emperor is Robbie Remus from Alpha Regulon!'

Later that day, a huge spaceship came
to pick up Robbie. It flew him halfway
across the galaxy to his new home, the
Royal Palace, on an ancient planet
called Earth.

A strict-looking woman met Robbie at the palace entrance.

'Greetings, Emperor Robbie. I am Miss Sourdust, your assistant,' she explained. 'It's my job to help you with your new duties.'

Robbie had thought that being Emperor might be fun, but after a few days he changed his mind. Miss Sourdust seemed more like his boss than his helper.

She was always telling Robbie what to do, or waking him up at the crack of dawn to inspect the Royal Guard. Once she made him spend the whole day travelling to the other end of the galaxy and back to open a new space station.

The worst thing about being Emperor was that Robbie had no time to play blasterball. There were no blasterball courts near the palace and ball games were not allowed in the Royal Gardens.

Once or twice, Robbie managed to sneak off to practise in one of the palace's vast banqueting halls. It wasn't like playing on a proper court with his teammates, but it was better than nothing.

'What are you doing up so early? And why are you dressed in that ridiculous way?' asked Miss Sourdust when Robbie came down for breakfast one morning. Robbie was wearing his Comets blasterball strip.

'It's the Junior League Final today!' explained Robbie. 'I'm leaving now so I can get to Alpha Regulon in time for blast-off!'

'Oh no you're not!' said Miss Sourdust. 'You're opening some new science buildings today, on Delta Megulon!'

The Duplitron

Three hours later, a very unhappy Robbie was being shown around some very shiny new science buildings.

Miss Sourdust had made him change out of his blasterball strip and into a stiff grey suit.

All sorts of strange scientific experiments were being carried out, but Robbie barely noticed.

He was still trying to convince Miss Sourdust to let him go to the blasterball match instead.

'My team will be expecting me! I can't

let them down. It's the final!' he explained.

'Your team have been told that you won't be playing today,' said Miss Sourdust firmly. 'I'm sure they'll understand that you have far better things to do. After all, you are the Emperor!'

They were halfway through the tour when they walked past an older, shabby-looking building. A big sign on the door said:

TOP SECRET
AUTHORISED PERSONS ONLY

'What's in there?' asked Robbie.

'That's Professor Parton's laboratory,' said Dr Drake, the scientist who was showing Robbie around. 'Even I'm not allowed in there. The professor is a brilliant scientist, but he won't tell anyone what he's working on.'

'Well, I think I'll take a quick look,' said Robbie.

'But Your Majesty,' protested Miss Sourdust. 'I don't think –'

'Nothing should be kept secret from me,' interrupted Robbie. 'After all, I *am* the Emperor!'

'I'm sure the Emperor could have a quick look,' said Dr Drake. 'But only the Emperor!'

Robbie could not believe how untidy it was inside the laboratory. The benches were piled high with equipment and half-empty food containers.

'Ready at last!' muttered a voice. Robbie spotted Professor Parton fiddling with the controls of a large machine.

The professor wore a lab coat, some boxer shorts and nothing else! Clearly he was not expecting visitors.

'Now to test it!' said the professor, taking a rat out of a cage.

He opened a glass door at one end of the machine and popped the rat inside. Then he pressed a big green button.

A humming sound filled the room. There was another glass door at the opposite end of the machine and behind it Robbie could see

a cloud of mist swirling around.

Finally the mist thinned. A second rat had appeared!

'That's brilliant!' shouted Robbie.

'It is, isn't it,' agreed the professor. Then he spun around in surprise.

'Who are you?' he demanded. 'And what are you doing in my laboratory?'

Robbie Repeats

'I'm Robbie,' said Robbie, 'and –'

'I don't care if you're the Emperor of the Galaxy,' snapped the professor. 'No one's allowed in here. It's top secret!'

'Well actually, I *am* the Emperor of the Galaxy,' said Robbie. 'And that means I can go wherever I like.'

'Oh. I do beg your pardon, Your Majesty,' the professor said. He quickly buttoned his lab coat to cover up his boxer shorts.

'And I'm really glad I came in here,' said Robbie. 'Your machine is amazing.'

'Thank you,' said the professor, glowing with pride. 'I call it the Duplitron.'

'It just made that rat, didn't it?' said Robbie.

'Yes, and it's not just any rat, Your Majesty,' said the professor, taking both rats out of the machine. 'The new rat is a clone of the first one. That means that it's an exact copy. And the Duplitron didn't just copy the first rat's body; it copied its mind and memories as well. So not only does this cloned rat *look* like the first one –'

'– It *thinks* like it too!' said Robbie.

'Exactly!' said the professor.

Suddenly Robbie had a thought. An exciting

and extraordinary thought. A thought that could help him escape his boring new life and get back to playing blasterball.

'So can the Duplitron clone any living thing? Any plant or animal?'

'Absolutely!' nodded the professor.

'So it could clone me!'

'Well, yes, I suppose it could,' said the professor, uncomfortably.

'Well, let's give it a try,' said Robbie.

'But Your Majesty,' said the professor, wringing his hands. 'I've only tested the machine on a rat. It would be far too risky to –'

'If you don't want to do as your Emperor wishes, that's up to you,' interrupted Robbie, innocently. 'But if you did, I might be able to get you one of those nice big shiny new laboratories . . .'

'Well, since you put it like that . . .' said the professor, '. . . would Your Majesty like to climb inside?'

Once Robbie had climbed into the Duplitron, the professor pushed the green button.

A moment later, Robbie felt a funny tingle go from the top of his head to the tip of his toes as the Duplitron scanned his whole body.

Then the professor opened the door again and Robbie climbed out.

Before Robbie could ask if it had worked, another Robbie climbed out of the other door.

'Snap!' said Emperor Robbie and his clone, Robbie Two, as their eyes met.

A Problem Shared

'*There* you are, Your Majesty. We're running late!' said Miss Sourdust impatiently, when Robbie finally came out of the lab.

'And who is this ridiculous person?' she asked, eyeing the scruffy-looking man who had followed Robbie out.

'This is my new friend, Professor Parton,' explained Robbie. 'I'm giving him one of the new labs, so I've invited him to come and look at them.'

Robbie and the professor walked off, leaving Miss Sourdust and Dr Drake speechless.

Back inside the professor's old laboratory, Robbie Two was far from happy. The Emperor had told his clone to stay there until he came back to collect him.

But Robbie Two had all of the Emperor's memories, so he knew exactly why he'd been created. It was so that he could do all of the royal duties while the real Emperor went off and played blasterball.

The problem was that Robbie Two was an exact copy of the Emperor, so he also hated the idea of doing boring duties.

'It's not fair,' Robbie Two said to himself. 'If only I could pass the job on to someone else.'

And then Robbie Two had a thought. An exciting and extraordinary thought . . .

When Robbie and the professor got back to the lab, instead of finding one Robbie clone, they found six. And they were all arguing with each other.

'Why should I have to do all the duties?' complained Robbie Seven.

'Because you're the new boy,' said Robbies Two, Three, Four, Five and Six, even though they'd only been around for a few minutes longer than Robbie Seven had.

'I can soon change that!' said Robbie Seven, opening the door of the Duplitron.

'Enough!' shouted Professor Parton, hitting the red button that shut down the machine. 'No more Robbies!'

'How dare you speak to me like that? I'm the Emperor!' said all six clones at once.

'No you're not. He is!' said the professor, pointing at Robbie. 'I knew this was a bad idea. I should never have let you talk me into it.'

'I just wanted one of them,' said Robbie, shaking his head in amazement. 'So that I could play blasterball.'

'Well I want to play blasterball too!' said all of the other Robbies.

'What is this "blasterball"?' asked Professor Parton.

So they told him all about it.

'Each team has six players,' said the professor thoughtfully. 'I think I have an answer to your problem . . .'

The Royal Robbies

A year later, the crowd in the arena went wild as the Emperor took his seat in the Royal Box.

Emperor Robbie grinned and waved back at them. This was one duty that he'd actually been looking forward to. He was here to watch the Galactic Cup Final.

Robbie's mum and dad were sitting with him, and so was Miss Sourdust.

Miss Sourdust had seen dozens of blasterball matches with Robbie in the last year. She was now a huge fan of the sport. Today she was dressed in her favourite team's strip and she was wearing a big frizzy red-and-blue wig.

'Come on you Royals!' she screamed as the two teams flew out into the arena.

Robbie Five was the Emperor today.

Professor Parton's brilliant idea was that each
of the Robbies should be Emperor for one
day every week. This meant the other six
were free to play blasterball. And six was just
enough to make their own blasterball team,
the Royal Robbies.

Robbie was a brilliant player, so six Robbies

were almost unbeatable. They'd only been playing for one season, but they had made it all the way to the Galactic Cup Final.

One reason the Royal Robbies made such a great team was because they all thought the same way, but sometimes that could be a

problem. Right now they were arguing with each other at one end of the court.

Robbie Five knew what they were arguing about. They argued about the same thing before every match. All of the Robbies liked playing in attack . . .

47

. . . so none of them wanted to be hole-keeper!